To Pete, Caitlin
  and the Mighty Huffer

First published 1999 by Walker Books Ltd
87 Vauxhall Walk, London SE11 5HJ

10 9 8 7 6 5 4 3 2

© 1999 Bob Graham

This book has been typeset in
Garamond Book Educational.

Printed in Hong Kong

British Library Cataloguing
in Publication Data
A catalogue record for this book is
available from the British Library.

ISBN 0-7445-6192-2

Buffy

An Adventure Story

Bob Graham

WALKER BOOKS
AND SUBSIDIARIES
LONDON • BOSTON • SYDNEY

Buffy had skills that were rare in a dog. As an assistant to Brillo the Magician, he did his job well enough…
But Buffy had talents all of his own.
He could juggle three clubs at once and throw a rope like a cowboy.

He could escape the
Houdini Deathtrap while
playing the harmonica.
"Bravo!" cried the audience.

His tap-dancing met with thunderous applause,
and how the dust rose from those well-trodden boards.

Brillo muttered darkly under his moustache.

Buffy was becoming more popular than him.

"OUT! and never come back," cried Brillo.

Buffy's bottom lip quivered with emotion
as he left the stage for ever.

He spent his last coins on a tin of dog food and a tin opener.

In a bleak railway yard he ate

the last of his Bonzo lamb chunks and pasta.

He wiped his mouth on his spotty scarf, and then …

Buffy jumped aboard
a moving freight train.

To the rhythm of the wheels,
he tapped his foot and sang,
"Oh, blue is me!
Oh, dearie me,
I'm as down as
A dog can be."

And while he slept, the train
continued its rhythm:
OUT, OUT …
and never come back.
OUT, OUT …
and never come back.

Buffy woke next morning to
the smell of fresh-cut grass
and countryside.

He put his harmonica in his
bag and leapt off the train.
"I will bring my tricks
to the world," he said.

But the world did not want Buffy's tricks. Nobody wanted a dancing sheep dog.

Nobody wanted a tiny rope-throwing cattle dog.

Nobody wanted a plate-juggling kitchen dog.

Nobody wanted
a guard dog
who played
the harmonica.

Only one person
wanted a wanderer
like Buffy ...

but Buffy did
not want him!

"I will find myself a home," he said,
and travelled the world.

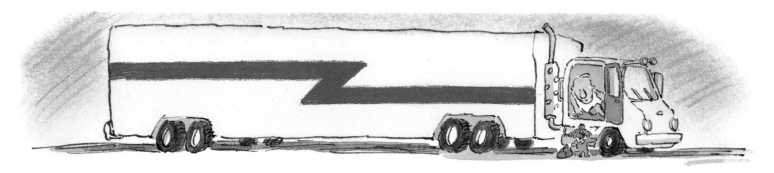

He sat above the roaring engines of mighty road trucks.

He crossed rivers,

and deserts.

He stood on
mountains and
moaned at
the moon.

Then one day Buffy stopped. He put down his bag,
wiped his brow and looked around him.

"I can go no further," he said.

"I'm not a sheep dog, a cattle dog, a kitchen dog
or a guard dog. So what sort of dog am I?"

"I am Buffy!
And I will do
what I do.
And this time,
the world shall
come to me."

Buffy's feet beat out the rhythm of the train on the tracks
and his harmonica howled like the desert wind and
pulsed like the engines of the mighty road trucks.

Many coins rattled into Buffy's cup that day and many faces passed by. Then someone stood in front of him. His breath stopped. His feet stopped. The sun came out.

It was Mary Kelly.

And Mary's mother   and her father   and her brother

and her grandma,   her grandad

and her baby sister,
Morag.

For Buffy, and the Kellys too,
it was love at first sight.
Off he went, the coins heavy in his cup.
At last, he had found a place to call home.

Now, each night after
dinner, the music starts
and each night the
floorboards shake.
Mary's and Buffy's feet
beat to the rhythm of
the jigs and the reels.

And Buffy lives up there,
on the hill, to this day.